Taking Autism To School

by Andreanna Edwards

Adapted for the
Special Kids in School® series
created by Kim Gosselin

JayJo Books, L.L.C.
Publishing Special Books for Special Kids®

Taking Autism to School
© 2001 JayJo Books, LLC
Edited by Kim Gosselin

Published by
JayJo Books, LLC
A Guidance Channel Company
Publishing Special Books for Special Kids®

JayJo Books is a publisher of books to help teachers, parents, and children cope with chronic illnesses, special needs, and health education in classroom, family, and social settings.

Library of Congress Control Number: 2001087641
ISBN 1-891383-13-2
First Edition
Tenth book in our *Special Kids in School*® series

For information about
Premium and Special Sales, contact:
JayJo Books Special Sales Office
P.O. Box 213
Valley Park, MO 63088-0213
636-861-1331
jayjobooks@aol.com
www.jayjo.com

For all other information, contact:
JayJo Books
A Guidance Channel Company
135 Dupont Street, P.O. Box 760
Plainview, NY 11803-0760
1-800-999-6884
jayjobooks@guidancechannel.com
www.jayjo.com

The opinions in this book are solely those of the author. Medical care is highly individualized and should never be altered without professional medical consultation.

About the Author

Andreanna Edwards is active with the Autism Society of North Carolina. She attended the University of Florida, receiving a B.S. degree in occupational therapy. As the author of Taking Autism to School, she was able to combine her educational background, dedication to those with special needs, and love of writing. Doing so fulfilled her desire to supply a much-needed tool for explaining a complicated disorder. Andreanna is also an active member of the Society of Children's Book Writers and Illustrators. She now resides in North Carolina.

Hi, boys and girls! My name is Angel. This is my friend, Sam. Sam and I are a lot alike. We live on the same street. We are in the same class at school. We both love animals too!

Lots of things about Sam and me are almost the same...

But many things about Sam and me are different. Sam lives with a condition called autism. Autism affects the way Sam talks, learns, acts, and feels. No one knows for sure what causes autism, but we do know it is not contagious. Sam can't give you, or anyone else, autism!

Sam didn't do anything wrong to cause his autism, and it's nobody's fault either!

Kids who have autism can learn new things and maybe even get better at them! In school, we have two teachers in our classroom, Mr. Post and Mrs. Jackson. Mrs. Jackson is Sam's special teacher. Her job is to give Sam extra help when he needs it. Sam and Mrs. Jackson made a daily chart with pictures and words on it. The chart tells Sam what he will do each day at school. He likes to know exactly what is going to happen. It also helps Sam if he only does one thing at a time. He usually learns best when there is not too much noise around him.

It helps Sam feel better when he knows what to expect.

Mrs. Jackson explained the human brain to our class. The brain is the part of our body we use to make sense of the world. Because Sam lives with autism, messages in his brain might get mixed up or confuse him. Because Sam's brain gets mixed-up messages, it's hard for him to talk or explain how he feels. Sam might have trouble understanding how other people feel too.

Everyone gets confused sometimes, but not everyone has autism.

For Sam, looking at someone's face might be like looking into a funny mirror at a county fair. What Sam sees may look strange or might not make any sense to him. This might be why Sam doesn't look directly into people's faces very much.

Sometimes Sam gets upset. Mrs. Jackson told me that kids with autism can be very sensitive to the world around them. Some sounds may bother Sam or hurt his ears. His clothes may suddenly feel scratchy on his skin. Even a funny smell may cause Sam to get upset.

Kids living with autism (like Sam) can be very sensitive to many things around them.

One day before lunch, our class was lined up in the cafeteria. Mrs. Jackson asked each kid if they wanted regular milk or chocolate milk. When she asked Sam, he copied exactly what she said.

"Would you like regular milk or chocolate milk?" Mrs. Jackson asked.

"Would you like regular milk or chocolate milk?" Sam said back to her. I thought Sam might get in trouble for being a copycat, but he didn't.

Later, Mrs. Jackson explained that this copying was just part of living with autism.

Next, Mrs. Jackson wrote the word "echo" on the chalkboard. "Echo" means to copy what someone says. Some kids with autism "echo" instead of saying their own words. When Sam "echoes" it's a way for him to tell us his feelings.

Sam can't help it when he echoes. He's not trying to be mean or funny.

Sometimes during recess, we invite Sam to play ball with us. Usually though, he would rather be alone. Sam sits by himself a lot. Sometimes, Sam rocks back and forth. This is another way he can express himself. Some kids who have autism repeat other things too. They might flap their hands over and over. They might play with toys by stacking them or spinning them over and over. Usually, kids living with autism like to do the same things at the same time each and every day.

Keeping on schedule might help Sam feel better.

Doing something over and over again is called "repetition." After Sam gets home from school, Sam always likes to eat a snack right away. Sam likes repetition.

Repetition is good for Sam!

Special medicines might help Sam feel better too. His doctors and nurses try to find the best medicines for him. It's very important for Sam to take his medicines at the same time each and every day. The school nurse and his family can help him remember!

It's very important for Sam's medicine to be part of his schedule!

Many doctors and other important people are learning new things about autism every day. Our class is learning more about autism too. The more we learn, the better we can understand Sam and his feelings. Understanding is what being friends is all about! I'm glad Sam is my friend.

I hope Sam can be your friend too!

LET'S TAKE THE AUTISM KIDS' QUIZ!

1. **Autism might affect the way someone:**
   A. talks
   B. learns
   C. acts
   D. feels
   E. all of the above
   E. all of the above

2. **True or false: You can catch autism from another person.**
   False. Autism is not contagious. You can't catch it from Sam or anyone else!

3. **What causes autism?**
   No one knows for sure, but doctors and other important people are studying autism. They are making new discoveries all the time.

4. **What can kids who have autism do to help themselves feel better?**
   They can take special medicines (with the help of their doctors and family, of course).

5. **Should you make fun of a classmate with autism?**
   No. Everyone has feelings. Everyone is different. Understanding each other's differences is what being friends is all about.

Great job! Thanks for taking the Autism Kids' Quiz!

TEN TIPS FOR TEACHERS

✔ **1. EACH CHILD LIVING WITH AUTISM IS DIFFERENT.**
Autism is often referred to as a spectrum disorder. Symptoms can present themselves in a variety of combinations. Two children diagnosed with autism may behave very differently from each other. The intensity of symptoms may also vary from extremely mild to severe.

✔ **2. EARLY TESTING FOR AUTISM IS IMPERATIVE.**
Autism typically appears during the first three years of life. Early diagnosis and intervention are vital to the child's development.

✔ **3. STOP, LOOK, AND LISTEN TO THE STUDENT WITH AUTISM.**
Agitated physical behaviors such as tantrums, increased repetitive movements, or odd vocalizations may indicate a basic problem. Does your student need to use the restroom? Is the classroom unusually noisy? Is the student frustrated with an activity? Does the student feel crowded by others?

✔ **4. ATTEMPT TO MODIFY CURRICULUM AND MATERIALS TO BEST SUIT THE STUDENT'S LEARNING STYLE.**
Many children with autism are visual learners and may benefit from the use of pictures and charts within the classroom. Whenever possible, practice skills in real situations (e.g., use real money when teaching monetary units and/or practice appropriate community behavior in the community).

✔ **5. ATTEMPT TO MODIFY THE CLASSROOM ENVIRONMENT TO BEST SUIT THE STUDENT'S NEEDS.**
Create an environment that minimizes distractions without isolating or secluding the child. Be sensitive to the autistic child's needs.

6. CONSTRUCT A UNIT ON HOW PEOPLE ARE DIFFERENT, ALIKE, AND SPECIAL.

Some people use wheelchairs or have hearing aids. Others have differences that are not easily seen, such as autism or diabetes. Our differences and our similarities make us special. Use these opportunities to teach about tolerance and empathy.

7. BECOME A TEAM PLAYER.

Cooperation between home and school is vital in the treatment of students with autism. Communicate with parents regularly, and include your school nurse as part of the team.

8. ENCOURAGE APPROPRIATE BEHAVIOR AND PREVENT SITUATIONS THAT MAY LEAD TO UNDESIRABLE BEHAVIOR.

Appropriate behavior can be increased in students with autism through the use of tangible rewards. Likewise, inappropriate behavior can often be averted through the use of consistency in schedules and activities.

9. DO NOT PUNISH THE CHILD FOR HAVING AUTISM.

Children with autism do not physically appear different from other students. But remember, children with autism may have extreme difficulties relating to and understanding the feelings of others.

10. EDUCATE OTHERS.

Education is the first step in working toward acceptance. Due to the complexity of autism, ignorance and misinformation often surround the disorder. It is important to convey that autism is a developmental disorder, not a psychosis.

ADDITIONAL RESOURCES

Autism Society of America
7910 Woodmont Avenue, Suite 300
Bethesda, MD 20814-3015
301-657-0881
800-328-8476
www.autism-society.org

Autism Research Institute
4182 Adams Avenue
San Diego, CA 92116
619-281-7165
www.autism.com/ari

Families for Early Autism Treatment
P.O. Box 255722
Sacramento, CA 95865-5722
916-843-1536
www.feat.org

The Autism Research Foundation
P.O. Box 1571, GMF
Boston, MA 02205
617-414-5286
www.ladders.org

National Institute of Mental Health
Public Inquiries
6001 Executive Boulevard
Room 8184, MSC 9663
Bethesda, MD 20892-9663
301-443-4573
www.nimh.nih.gov

To order additional copies of *Taking Autism to School* or inquire about our quantity discounts for schools, hospitals, and affiliated organizations, contact us at 1-800-999-6884.

From our *Special Kids in School*® series

Taking A.D.D. to School
Taking Asthma to School
Taking Cancer to School
Taking Cerebral Palsy to School
Taking Cystic Fibrosis to School
Taking Diabetes to School
Taking Food Allergies to School
Taking Seizure Disorders to School
Taking Tourette Syndrome to School
... and others coming soon!

From our new *Healthy Habits for Kids*™ series

There's a Louse in My House
A Fun Story about Kids and Head Lice

Coming soon ...
Playtime Is Exercise!
A Fun Story about Exercise and Play

From our new *Special Family and Friends*™ series

Allie Learns about Alzheimer's Disease
A Family Story about Love, Patience, and Acceptance
... and others coming soon!

Other books available now!

SPORTSercise!
A School Story about Exercise-Induced Asthma

ZooAllergy
A Fun Story about Allergy and Asthma Triggers

Rufus Comes Home
Rufus the Bear with Diabetes™
A Story about Diagnosis and Acceptance

The ABC's of Asthma
An Asthma Alphabet Book for Kids of All Ages

Taming the Diabetes Dragon
A Story about Living Better with Diabetes

Trick-or-Treat for Diabetes
A Halloween Story for Kids Living with Diabetes

And from our *Substance Free Kids*® series

Smoking STINKS!! ™
A Heartwarming Story about the Importance of Avoiding Tobacco

A portion of the proceeds from all our publications is donated to various charities to help fund important medical research and education. We work hard to make a difference in the lives of children with chronic conditions and/or special needs. Thank you for your support.